A course in drawing for young people

THE INCREDIBLE, SPREADABLE, MAGIC, DRAWING BOOK

Wayne Dean 1983

Fourth Printing, 1987

©1983 Wayne Dean
Editorial Advisor, Leven C. Leatherbury
Editor, L. Diana Harryman

Wayne Dean Editions, 3217 Petunia Court, San Diego, California 92117

ISBN 0-9616161-0-5 8.95

LOOKING AND SEEING

"A drawing is an idea with a line around it." This perceptive statement was made by a child in elementary school. Young people can draw anything from a rocket to a view of the other side of the moon, while most adults think that they are unable to draw a straight line. This book presents a series of exercises designed to develop **your drawing skills,** whatever your age.

You want to learn to draw! The basic elements in drawing are **learning to see** and **lots of practice.** By following the suggestions presented and doing each of the exercises, you will develop your own drawing skills.

3

This book is organized to help you understand that drawing is based upon observation. The activities are arranged to help you learn to draw using contour, tone, and gesture techniques.

Ideas from recent brain hemisphere research are also stressed. You will learn that you can draw better if you are relaxed, confident and quiet. You will tend to avoid talking while drawing and avoid those who do. You may find that soft instrumental music will help you concentrate as you draw.

Courtesy of the San Diego Museum of Art.

4

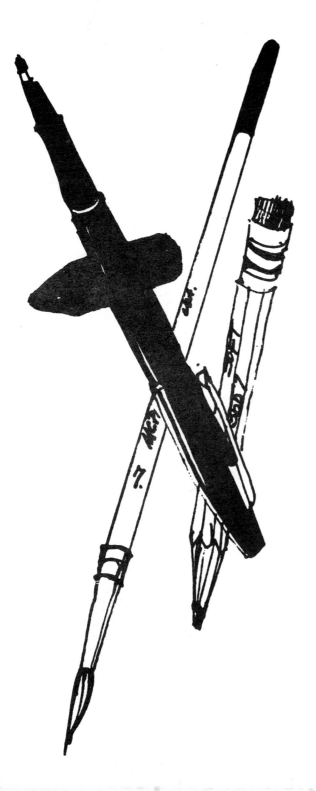

You will need a fine-line, black felt-tip pen; a black crayon; a soft pencil; a small, pointed #7 brush; a watercolor box; and an inexpensive sketchbook or sheets of paper at least as large as this page.

Set aside time for drawing every day. Drawing depends upon practice, just as basketball, typing, or playing the piano. Make a habit of carrying your sketchbook with you. Do at least two small drawings each day.

Let's see how well you draw now. To check your ability, draw the following subjects on one piece of paper: a face, a house, and a television set.

Which drawing was easiest for you? Most people agree that a television set is easy to draw. Why do you think this is so? Experts tell us that we spend more time watching television than any other activity except sleeping. Thousands of hours spent looking at television sets have made them easier to draw.

Most people draw objects the same way again and again because they draw the pictures they see in their mind. These *mind pictures* are called mental images. Although mental images are helpful to us in many ways, they can also trick us into doing simple and inaccurate drawings when we are first learning to draw.

Make a drawing using a mental image. Close your eyes and think of a bicycle. Now draw it. From time to time, close your eyes and use your mental image of the bicycle to help you add details to your drawing. When you next ride a bicycle, study it carefully. It will help you when you draw it again.

This book is filled with drawings by artists of all ages. The drawings show that **there is no one correct way to draw.** As you do the exercises that follow, you will be shown different ways to create your own unique drawings: using your mental images, using your imagination, and most important, using your ability to observe.

The trick in learning to draw is **learning to see!** This means learning to see the world clearly without letting words and your mental images get in the way. It means seeing and drawing in your own special way.

To begin, find a leaf that has a complicated shape and many details. Observe the leaf carefully. Place it out of sight. Now draw the leaf from memory.

7

If there is a secret to drawing, it is in looking very carefully at the object you are drawing. Now, hold the same leaf in one hand and begin to draw carefully while looking at it. Make sure your pen describes the leaf's shape, its veins, stem, and texture. Compare your two leaf drawings. Which do **you** think is better? Which drawing tells most about the leaf?

Compare the leaf drawings you have made with these leaves drawn by Brett, Brian, and David. Observe carefully as you draw other types of leaves.

8

Notice Billy's striking drawing of Uncle Sam. Billy first drew the hat and then drew the face. Notice that the head appears too large for the hat. The mis-match in the sizes of the hat and head results in a unique image. Such an accident can happen if you do not look again and again at the object you are drawing.

Let's try two more drawings.
● Draw a goldfish from memory.
● Now find a real goldfish. Look at the goldfish for 2 or 3 minutes and then make a drawing as you watch it swim. If a goldfish is hard to find, draw a pine cone, or a flower, or insect first from memory and then from the real thing. Remember, first draw from memory, then draw while looking carefully at the subject.

9

Sandy, Suzy, and Ferdy each drew a goldfish twice. First they sketched a fish from memory, then they made a drawing while looking at a goldfish in a jar. Which drawings do you think look **most "fish"-like? ***

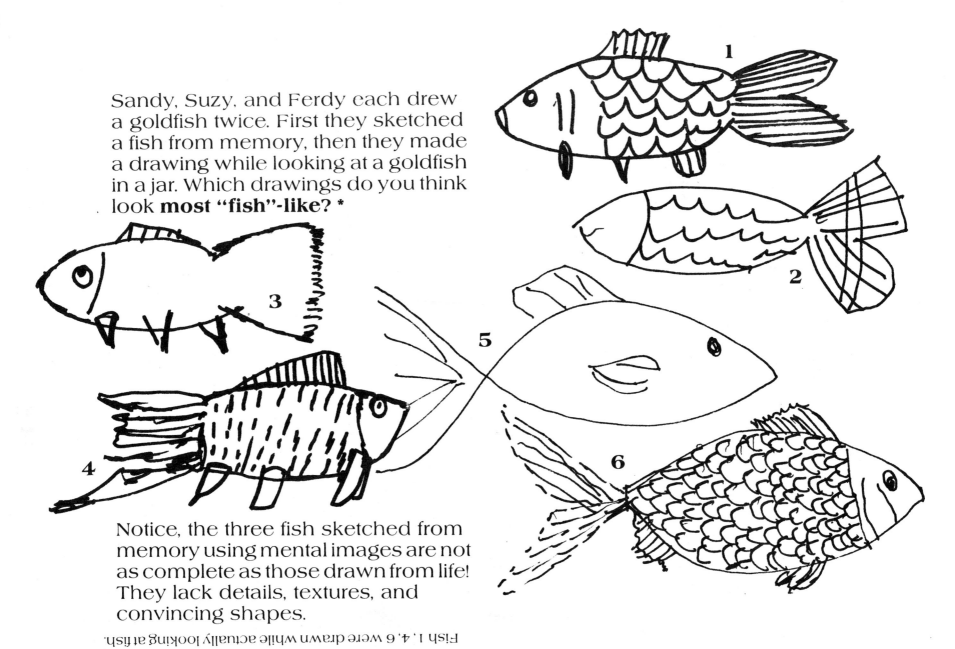

Notice, the three fish sketched from memory using mental images are not as complete as those drawn from life! They lack details, textures, and convincing shapes.

Fish 1, 4, 6 were drawn while actually looking at fish.

Perhaps drawing is no more than copying something with care, in your own way. Seeing all the details is very important.

Make an **add-on drawing** of this rooster. Draw him with a pencil in a new way!

- Start with the rooster's tail and draw each feather.
- Add his legs, feet and claws.
- Draw the ruff at his neck.
- Locate his eye on the paper, then complete his head and comb.
- Finish the drawing, adding as many details as you can see.

It may help you to concentrate while drawing if soft instrumental music can be playing in the background.

Toys are great to draw, whatever
your age. These toys were drawn by
Kori and Jill as they carefully
observed each detail. Notice the
patterns that have been added to
Raggedy Ann's blouse and stockings.

Find a complicated toy and draw it
with care using a felt pen. **Look for
patterns** that can be added to your
drawing. Draw the same toy again
from a different angle.

Look again and again at the toy as you draw!

These felt pen portraits of George Washington were done while looking at a picture. Find a photograph of a famous person and **make a portrait.**

Begin with the eyes from the center as you your drawing by outlir and filling in all details

Expressive drawings can also be the bases for personalized note cards! Heather's George Washington is a fine example.

Holiday cards are a wonderful way to use your drawings. Lisa's Pegasus above and Heather's George Washington were printed on heavy, colored stock. A black ink drawing and black letters on white paper can be combined to make a card at a quick print shop.

A Heather Card – Artist age 6

Thousands of drawings based on careful observations of plants, animals, men, and machines were made by Leonardo da Vinci almost 500 years ago! This famous artist-inventor constantly studied the world around him, making sketches and recording ideas in his famous notebooks. Da Vinci made hundreds of drawings because he recognized that doing many drawings helps a person know any subject well.

Find a live snail or insect. Place it in front of you and draw it as many times as Da Vinci drew these cats. Use a pencil for your renderings.

Courtesy of The Royal Library, Windsor Castle, copyright reserved.

CONTOUR DRAWING

Contours are lines that go around shapes. The car, the people, the parts of the car, and the shadows all have outline edges that you can see. Notice that you can also see other lines — spokes and poles.

The trick is to see all the contours! If you draw all of these edges and lines, you have made a **contour** drawing. There is no shading in a contour drawing… only outlines. The tracing shows how some lines describing the edges of shapes can become lost against other shapes.

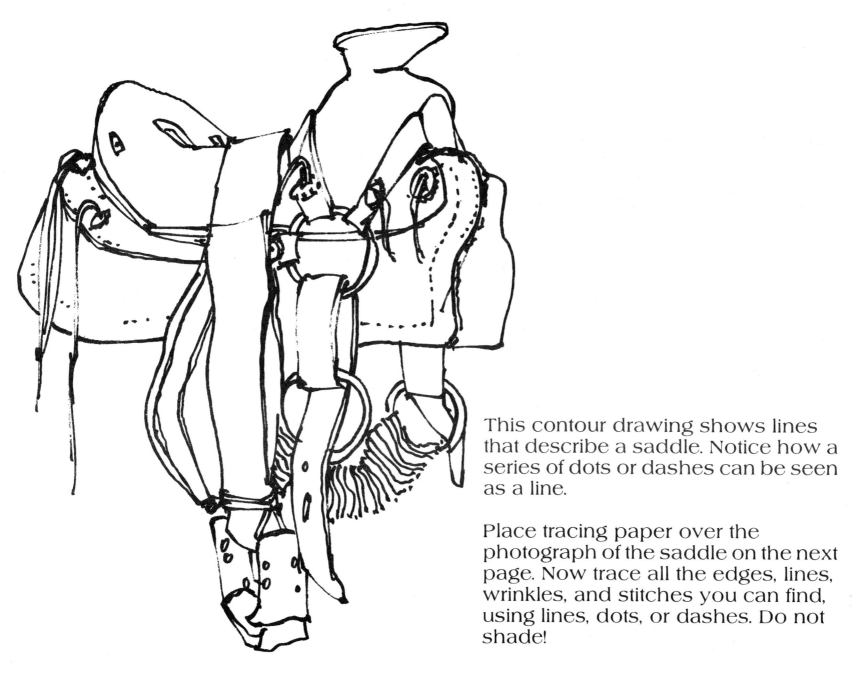

This contour drawing shows lines that describe a saddle. Notice how a series of dots or dashes can be seen as a line.

Place tracing paper over the photograph of the saddle on the next page. Now trace all the edges, lines, wrinkles, and stitches you can find, using lines, dots, or dashes. Do not shade!

Tracing is not creative drawing.
However, tracing can sometimes help you to see more shapes and details than your mental images include.

Now make a contour drawing of the saddle, twice as large as the photograph. Using your pen, start with the large ring near the center of the saddle. Make your drawing grow from the center out. Draw all the edges, lines, and shapes that you can find. Do not shade.

BLIND CONTOURS

One important way to learn to see is called **blind contour drawing.** You will need a ballpoint pen, a paper mask that covers the top of your hand, and the courage to draw without seeing your paper.

To make a mask, push a small hole into the center of an 8" x 8" piece of paper. Push your pen halfway through the paper. Then hold the pen below the paper. You will be unable to see the lines that you draw!

Place a flower on the table and look at it carefully. Begin a careful drawing of the flower. Of course, **you won't see what your pen is doing!** Draw each petal, stem, and leaf slowly.

Make your eye travel at the same pace and place over the flower as your pen travels the paper. Press hard. See and draw each contour, curve and edge. Do not lift your pen.

1

2

Which drawing was made blind? Of course, drawing #1 was done using the blind technique. No one can make blind drawings in proportion – but no one has found a better way to study what an object looks like!

This time look at the flower while drawing. Remove your mask from the pen. Keep the flower in the same position. Place your paper close to the flower and draw slowly and carefully as before. Make your eyes travel over the flower at the same place, as your pen moves over the paper, **but this time look at both the flower and the drawing.** Try to look at the flower's contours more than your drawing.

Experience indicates that a blind contour drawing adds information to our memory that improves a second contour drawing.

21

Observe the photograph at the right. Place drawing paper on this page just below the picture of the keys. Look at both the photograph and the pen as you make a contour drawing of the keys. Try to see a particular edge or line as you draw. Press firmly with your pen. Observe carefully and draw slowly.

Small objects can be placed right on your paper and drawn while looking at both the object and your pen.

Now try a drawing of you own keys. Place several keys on a sheet of drawing paper. Make a blind contour drawing using the paper mask. Next, make another contour drawing of the keys without the mask. This second drawing should be better than the first, because of your careful observation in doing a **blind** drawing of the keys.

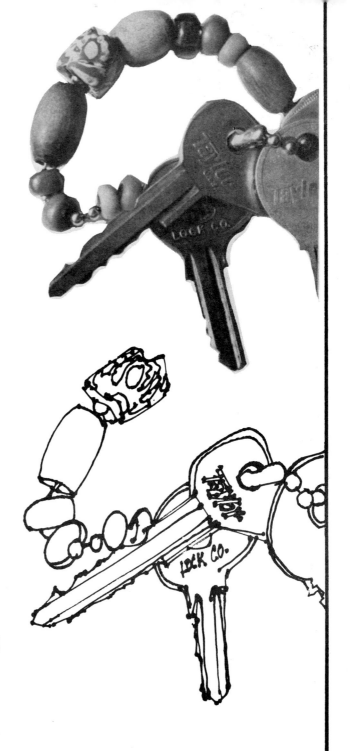

Drawing people in costume is an interesting way to practice contour drawing. Mark and Tina made these drawings of a classmate dressed in costume.

- Models in Western, sports, or Halloween dress are exciting to draw.
- It is best if the model can sit or lean against something for comfort.
- Try a profile view, then an overhead view by having the model sit on the floor.
- For variety, pose two people together.

Notice that a figure drawing need not show the entire person to be effective!

Over 75 years ago, a famous English artist, Aubrey Beardsley, used contour lines and areas of black ink to make very striking illustrations. Study the way Beardsley created several large areas of black and white and how carefully he drew all of the jewelry, leaving the white details on the black areas.

Make a drawing of the prince's hat, leaving the white of the paper for the beads and jewels as Beardsley has done.

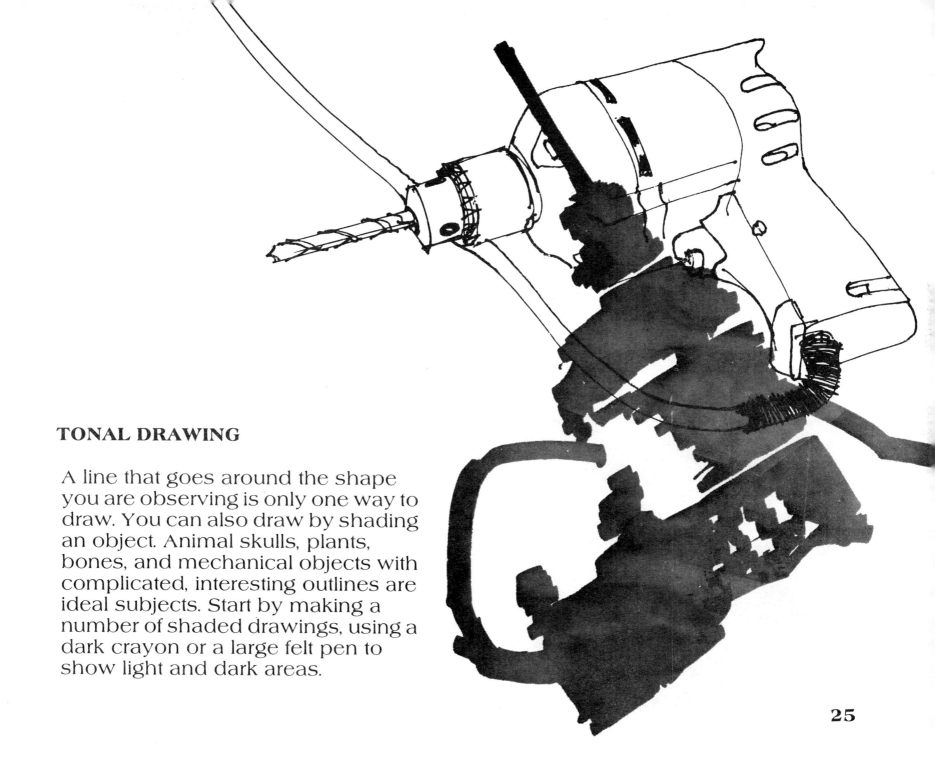

TONAL DRAWING

A line that goes around the shape you are observing is only one way to draw. You can also draw by shading an object. Animal skulls, plants, bones, and mechanical objects with complicated, interesting outlines are ideal subjects. Start by making a number of shaded drawings, using a dark crayon or a large felt pen to show light and dark areas.

One way to practice shading is to make rubbings of textured objects. Coins, weathered wood, and embossed designs on metal and cardboard are good subjects. Use a pencil or a crayon to do several small rubbings.

Shading is not the only way to create tone. A variety of line and textural patterns can be developed. Divide a circle into ten shapes and create a variety of tonal patterns by using lines, dots, cross hatching or solids.

Venice Italy 20
W. DEAN

A pencil rubbing of letters cut into the stone and bronze of the building was the first step in this drawing of Saint Mark's Basilica in Venice, Italy. Pen and pencil were next used to describe the building's contours. Then, areas of tone were used to complete the drawing.

People can be drawn with shading alone. Place tissue or tracing paper over this page. Use a soft pencil to shade in the figures. Don't draw lines!

Lightly shade a silhouette of one figure. Go back and darken it by re-shading the areas of the figure that are darkest in the picture. Do not draw lines!

Scribble figures are a fun method of learning the proportions of the human body.

Pose a model. Scribble short, quick, back-and-forth lines placed close together to shade in a shape or silhouette. Observe carefully and work fast. Use no more than 10 seconds per pose.

- Scribble the head.
- Skip the neck.
- Scribble the torso.
- Scribble the legs and feet.
- Add the arms.
- Draw any props with lines.

Remember, work fast!
Keep your drawings **small**.
Do not make the heads too large!

29

Of course the easiest way to make
tonal figure drawings is with a brush.

Use a small pointed brush and watercolor to puddle in the head and body
parts in one dull color. Do not draw
lines! Keep your work about the size
of the figures on this page, or smaller.

Painted figures of this type, with a
detail added here and there, populate
many an artist's paintings.

A good way to **see tonal shapes** clearly is by looking at shadows. Another way to draw tonal shapes is to place a complicated object, like a pair of eyeglasses, on a sheet of white paper, in strong light, and then shade its shadow with a soft pencil.

Tonal drawings made this way are interesting since the drawings are always distorted. Make several tonal drawings using this technique. Choose objects with complicated shapes. Look through your kitchen drawer for subjects to draw.

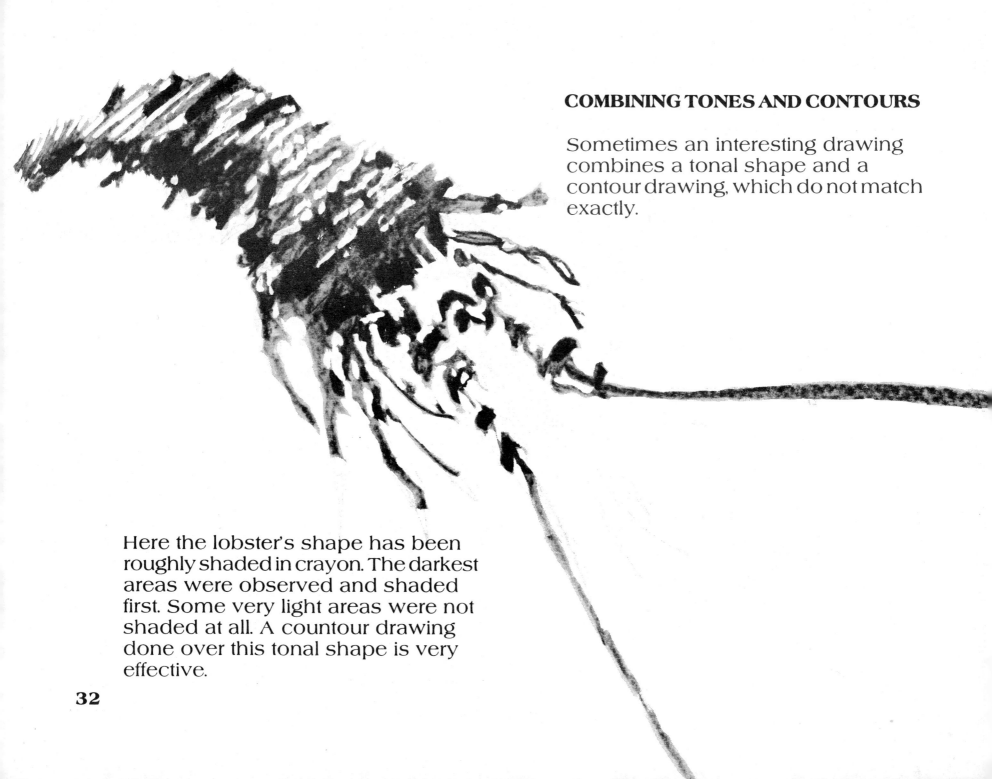

COMBINING TONES AND CONTOURS

Sometimes an interesting drawing combines a tonal shape and a contour drawing, which do not match exactly.

Here the lobster's shape has been roughly shaded in crayon. The darkest areas were observed and shaded first. Some very light areas were not shaded at all. A countour drawing done over this tonal shape is very effective.

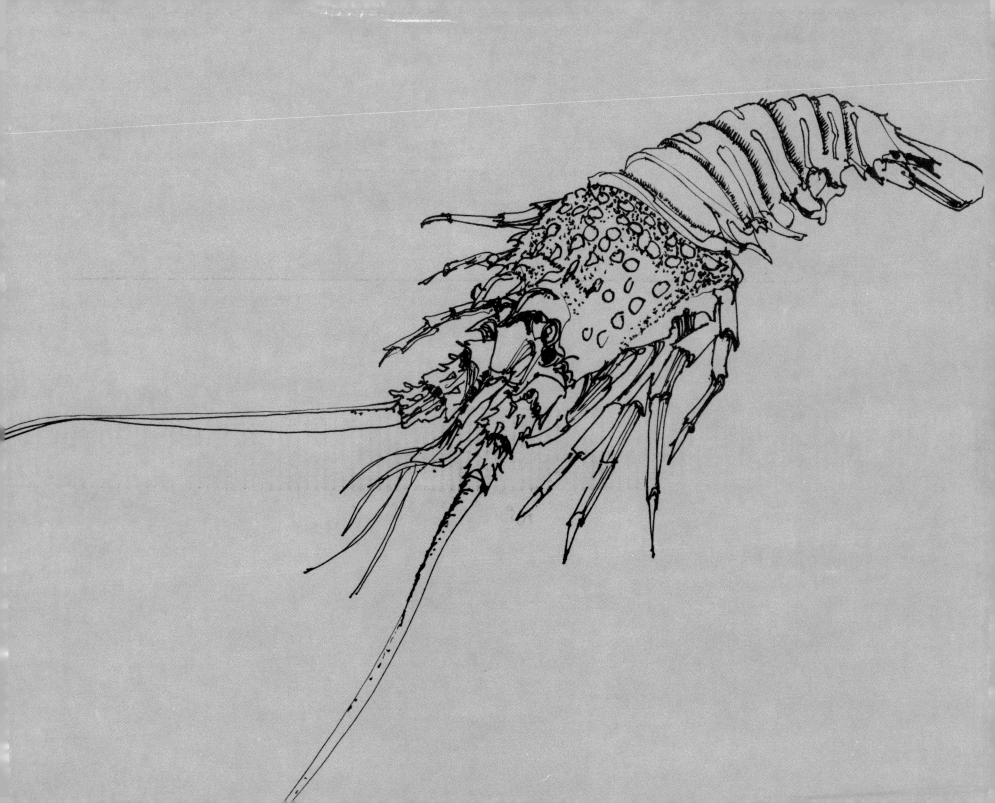

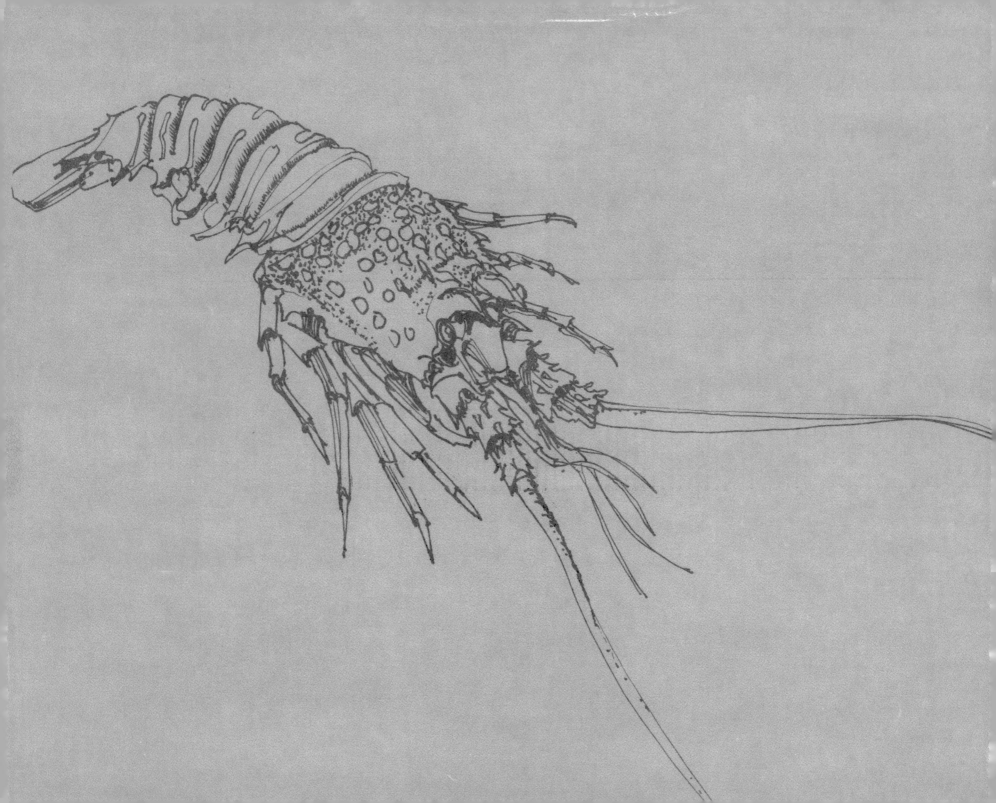

The background has been darkened
to reveal the lobsters' shape here.
Torn paper and masking tape were
assembled on drawing paper, then
lightly dusted with spray paint. When
removed, the lobsters shape is
revealed ready for a contour drawing.

33

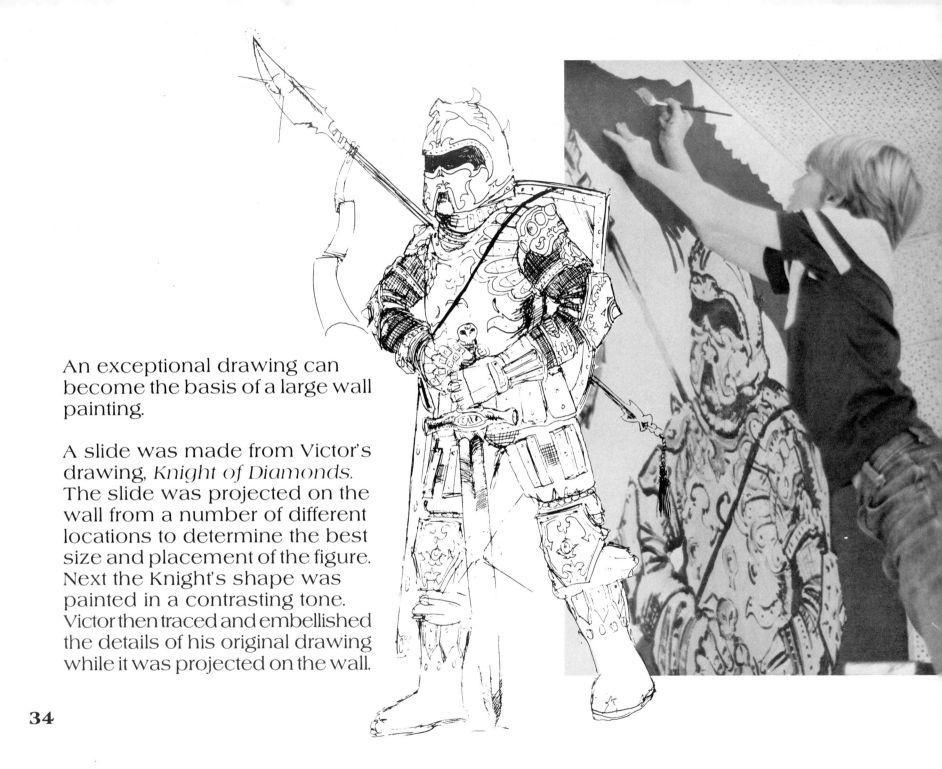

An exceptional drawing can become the basis of a large wall painting.

A slide was made from Victor's drawing, *Knight of Diamonds.* The slide was projected on the wall from a number of different locations to determine the best size and placement of the figure. Next the Knight's shape was painted in a contrasting tone. Victor then traced and embellished the details of his original drawing while it was projected on the wall.

34

Look at pictures in magazines and newspapers, using a magnifying glass. See how images are made from patterns of dots which are placed close together to form dark tones or far apart for lighter tones.

Find a lemon or a strawberry. Using a felt-tip pen, draw only points or dots to depict what you see. Observe carefully! Use very few lines! Apply more dots where the object is darker. Keep these drawings small, since this technique is time-consuming.

35

Use a felt-tip pen to draw these trees. Make only dots or short pen strokes to describe the foliage. Use many overlapping strokes in the dark areas. Make sure your strokes follow the direction of the lines in the trees.

Go outside and make several small drawings of trees viewed against the sky. Use dots or short pen strokes for the pattern of the foliage and just a few accurately drawn lines for the tree trunks.

Ed, a young surfer, used hundreds of dots to bring life to a simple drawing. Make a **small** drawing of a scene you like. Bring your drawing to life! Create a variety of tones with patterns made by a fine-line feltpen.

If you can visit a library or an art museum, try to see some works by American artist Chuck Close. He has used a similar "stippling" technique to produce very large portraits.

37

Finding subjects to draw may seem difficult at first. Not everyone is turned on by the same things. Think of your own interests. If you enjoy sports, try drawing sports equipment or people who are watching a sports event. A person who loves boats may make hundreds of drawings of boats, ships, and nautical gear.

Look at things up close, from underneath, or from the top. Look down at your feet right now. Could what you see be the subject for a drawing? Look up under a tree or at a utility pole and wires high in the skyline. Observe the weeds, the plants, and the sprinklers in a garden. A dented can or the items in your lunch sack all could become drawings.

The well-known artist, Robert Miles Parker, has traveled throughout the world drawing the structures that form our architectural heritage. *Roll-A Coaster* is an unusual and complex drawing of an offbeat subject.

From the collection of John Pritchard, San Diego.

GESTURE DRAWING

Gesture drawing is the opposite of contour drawing. Gesture is based more on feeling than upon observation. These "blind" gesture drawings are based entirely upon reaction to sound. No particular image or idea was intended. While perfectly relaxed, one merely moves the pen to music with the eyes closed.

Which drawing do you think was made while moving the pen to slower music?

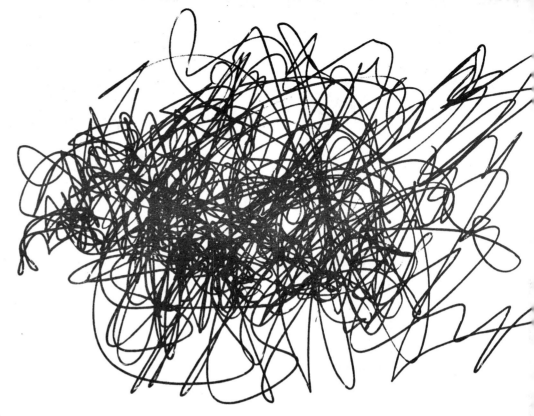

Make a blind drawing to music yourself. Close your eyes, relax, breath deeply several times, and draw while listening to music. Try several different drawings using a variety of music. Let your hand react. Concentrate on movement, not on realistic objects or ideas.

Gesture drawings capture action and movement, not detail. Sports events and dancing are great subjects that can be observed on your television.

Your first gesture drawings should be very abstract, almost as abstract as the drawings made from listening to music. Work quickly. Try for the **feel** of the action – nothing too recognizable. Concentrate on observing the action. Keep your pen moving. Do several drawings.

Try gesture drawing while looking at still photographs of people in action. Force yourself to work fairly rapidly! Ignore details and try for the main flow of movement. Make your work about twice the size of the drawings on this page. Do at least 10 sketches each time you try this type of drawing.

Gesture drawings are important and beautiful in themselves. They can also be the basis for more finished drawings where life and movement are essential.

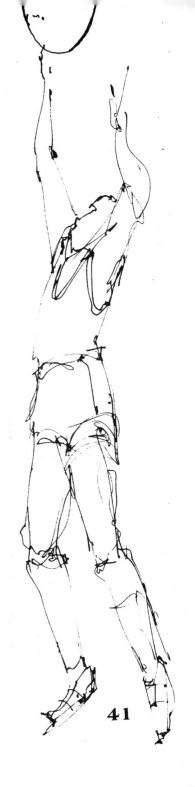

Drawing allows us to picture things we can only imagine . . . a huge, fat animal that has three horns and whiskers, a tattered tail and tiny wings. Draw such an animal of your own.

This is an Eskimo ghost spirit drawing. It probably does not fit your idea of what a ghost looks like at all. See if you can make a drawing of a ghost that is different from the conventional Halloween ghost image.

* Indicates image is a rendering by Richard Huber from *Treasury of Fantastic & Mythological Creatures.* Dover Publications, Inc.

42

*1   *2   *3

You can begin to see the unlimited possibilities of the imagination by studying the designs of other cultures. Ask your librarian to help you find books on the arts of Africa, Asia, and the Americas. Study the fantastic variety of styles that different cultures have developed.

Compare the ways animals and people have been depicted. On this page we see 1) an Egyptian tomb painting, 2) Mexican Aztec Gods, and 3) an American Indian killer whale.

Drawing allows us to dream, change and to distort time and the shape of things. Here Don, a young artist shows us part of a humorous story he created about the Revolutionary War in 1776. It involves a soldier with fire crackers going off in his hat and pocket, who steps on bubble gum in the road. Don

had drawn over 200 booklets with his own illustrated stories by age 11.

Create a short story of your own with several drawings in the style with which you are most comfortable. Set your story in another place and at a time other then the present.

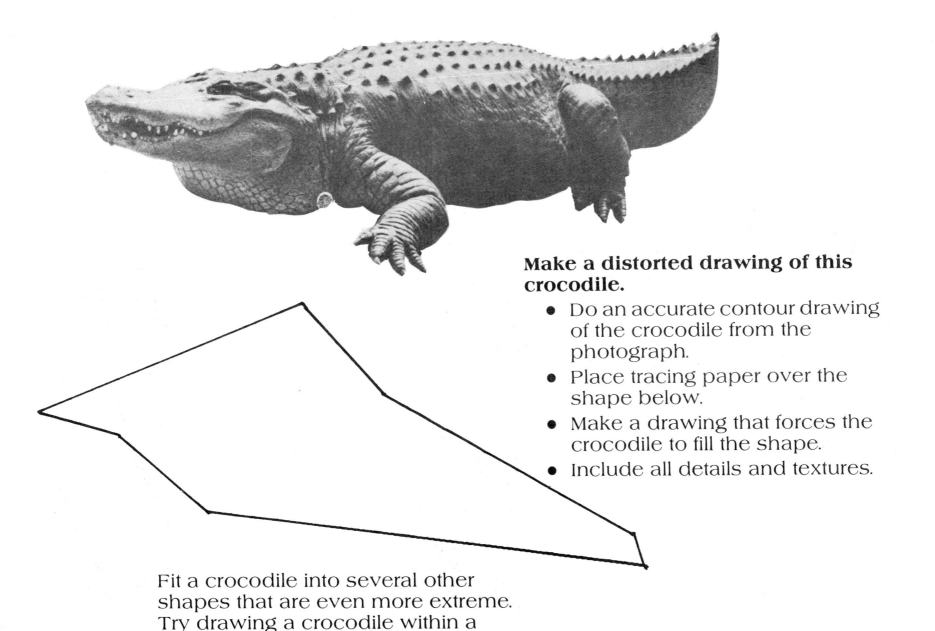

Make a distorted drawing of this crocodile.

- Do an accurate contour drawing of the crocodile from the photograph.
- Place tracing paper over the shape below.
- Make a drawing that forces the crocodile to fill the shape.
- Include all details and textures.

Fit a crocodile into several other shapes that are even more extreme. Try drawing a crocodile within a circle.

METAMORPHIC DRAWINGS

Metamorphic drawings are based upon change. Robert has caused his spacewarrior to become a flower upon a stem. Imagination is at work here.

Can you make a bee become a burro, or perhaps a ship become a shark? Draw the first and last images and then imagine the changes that take place as you create the intermediate images.

Robert Jones '82

Art that is conceived and planned largely in the mind is called **Conceptual Art.**

Sol Lewitt is an American artist who has created hundreds of Conceptional drawings. He explains, "When an artist uses a conceptual form of art all planning and decisions are made before hand. . ..The idea becomes a machine that makes the art." Study his drawing and its title.

Sol Lewitt believes that the **idea** is the most important part of the artwork and that the **idea** should be interesting to the viewer. What the artwork looks like is not too important! Another of Lewitt's drawings is titled, *VERTICAL LINES, NOT STRAIGHT, NOT TOUCHING.* Use a fine-line pen on 8" X 8" paper to make your own version of this drawing.

Successive Rows Of Horizontal, Straight Lines From Top To Bottom, And Vertical, Straight Lines From Left To Right,
Pen and Ink, 1972   Courtesy of the artist

Today, artists work in many ways using many different materials and tools.

- Some artists create **Representational Art** – art that usually describes the "real" world closely and realistically.

- Other artists create **Abstract Art** — art that usually changes or distorts the "real" world but is still often recognizable.

- Other artists create **Non-Objective Art** — art that adds new ideas and images to our world; that is, things never before seen.

Study the drawings on pages 4, 44 and 47. Decide which type of art is on each page.

EGYPT
RUSSIA
AFRICA
BLACKFOOT PLAINS INDIAN
SUDAN

48

For thousands of years artists have used drawings to describe their world or their ideas. A drawing by the German artist Albrecht Dürer was the basis for this woodcut. It was made over 450 years ago to celebrate a victory of his emperor, Maximilian.

From *The Triumph of Maximilian I.* Dover Publications Inc.

Mike, a young student, made this drawing of an undersea research vessel. It is very complete. His original design is well thought out and imaginative. He is adding something new to his world with his ideas.

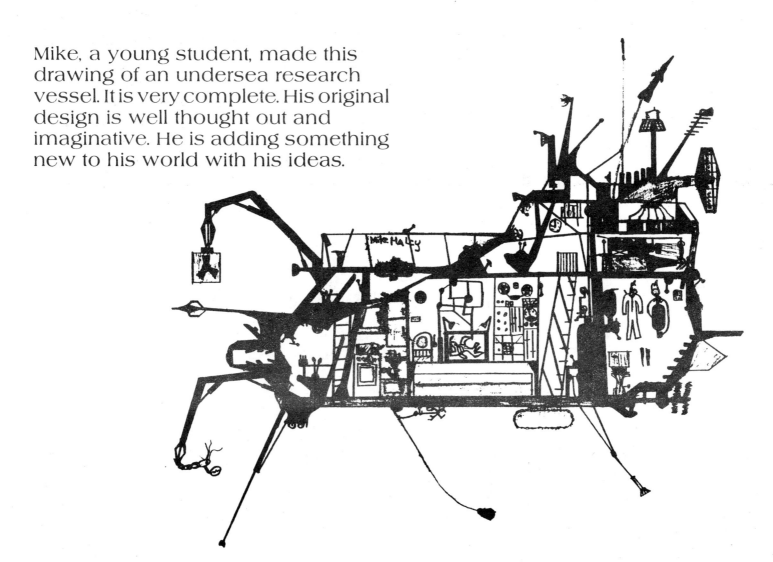

Make a drawing that describes your world. Put a line around one of **your** ideas.

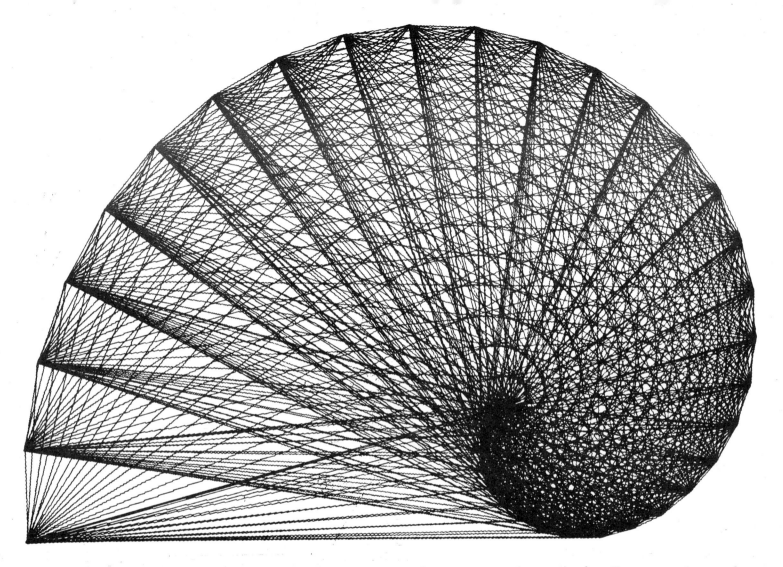

William, a junior high school student, put lines around one of his ideas by using mathematics to program a computer to make this drawing. His design is titled:

Nautilus 1, Designated – Connect Points Program 2, Program Revision III, 360° Archimedes Spiral with a 36 – 37 Point Connection.

Selected Bibliography for Teachers

Gerald F. Brommer. *Drawing: Ideas, Materials and Techniques.*
Davis Publications, Worcester, Mass., 1972. An excellent resource for high school art teachers, illustrated with the work of students and artists.

Betty Edwards. *Drawing on the Right Side of the Brain.*
J.P. Tracher Inc., Los Angeles, Calif., 1979. A paperback on drawing instruction based upon brain hemisphere research. Instructional theory and practice are illustrated by student work.

Daniel M. Mendelowitz. *Drawing.* Holt, Reinhart and Winston, Inc., New York, 1967. A very comprehensive history of drawing styles and techniques illustrated by the works of master artists.

Kimon Nicolaïdes. *The Natural Way To Draw.* Houghton Mifflin Co., Boston, Mass, 1941. A classic series of exercises designed as a complete program of drawing instruction for adults.

Frank Wachowiak and David Hodge. *Art in Depth.* International Textbook Co., Scranton, Penn., 1970. A guide to art instruction at the junior high level. Chapters on drawing instruction are illustrated with student work.

SUGGESTIONS FOR TEACHERS

4. The statement that anyone can learn to draw is trite but true. Recent research on the capacities of the brain indicate that the visual, spatial, Gestalt right hemisphere can accomplish amazing drawing feats if we allow ourselves and students to turn off our overexercised verbal, symbolic left hemispheres. If students can be persuaded to draw what they see, rather than what they know, immediate progress can be achieved. Young people who are able to describe the world around them in drawings are also better prepared to distort and create imaginative drawings completely of their own invention.

5. The new fine-line pens are a wonderful drawing instrument. Students should use them for most drawings since the pen line is crisp and emphatic. Students should become used to the idea of making many drawings rather than one drawing that aims to be a finished work of art. The pencil is a fascinating drawing instrument; however, early pencil work is often a series of false starts and erasures.

6. Give this simple test to your students and compare the results. You are sure to find some students who make more complete images than others.

8. Complicated leaves are best. Some students will try to trace the shape. Help them to see and record details. Do not shade!

9. Four or five goldfish each in a jar can be placed close to the student. This makes for a great drawing lesson. Don't bring them out until your students have made a drawing from memory. Urge them to study the fish! Point out the fins, scales, gills and all observable details. Urge, plead, entice them to look at the fish again and again.

11. Students must be reminded again and again to look at the object being drawn or they revert to drawing their mental image, not the object. Insist on complete quiet as students draw. Brain research shows that we cannot talk and do optimal visual work at the same time. Soft instrumental music will help.

12. Toys that are somewhat complicated are most suitable. Dolls, vehicles, boats and antique toys all offer possibilities. A light pencil drawing that describes the proportions of a complex toy is a good idea. Do not be surprised if students resist the idea of switching back to the pen to complete the drawing.

13. Save and date these early drawings for later reference. Compare results of your students with the drawings of nine-year-olds on this page.

Your main task in teaching at this stage is to urge students to look at the object again and again and again. Insist on quiet! Play soft classical or jazz music!

14. If you are not familiar with the offset printing process, visit a quick print shop with several drawings, for advice.

15. Acquire a book on Leonardo da Vinci and acquaint your students with some of the achievements of this giant of the Renaissance. His powers of imagination and observation were unequaled.

16. When beginning to draw in contour, one must help the student "let go" of preconceived mental images. It sometimes helps to project a slide from nature and, as a group, have students trace with a finger and then pen, all the contour lines and details they can discern. Do not shade.

18. A student may learn from a tracing now and then, as suggested, as long as the result is not passed as an original, creative drawing. Here, the purpose is to make the student aware of the numerous contours and lines to be found in the subject, without dealing with the problem of proportion.

19. After doing the exercises on these pages, it would be ideal to have a saddle to touch, smell, see, and become acquainted with. A number of drawings done from various angles would be beneficial. Urge students to start their drawings on some detail in the center of the composition, then work their way out to the drawing's boundaries. This forces one to draw what is actually seen and

not simply an image carried in the mind.

20. Blind contour drawings are an exercise in seeing. Urge students to draw slowly and deliberately. Demonstrate at the chalkboard.

23. The model should be elevated so that all can see. Occasionally masks, odd clothing, or unusual poses will add interest.

24. As students continue to draw, their sense of proportion will improve. Students need to see many examples of artists' drawings as they improve their own drawing skills. An eclectic display of drawings discovered by students in magazines is an excellent supplement to art books.

25. Just as with contour and line drawings, the student needs to observe actual objects as subject matter for drawings created in tone. Animal skulls, potted plants, shells, bones, and mechanical objects with interesting outlines are ideal. Books, balls, and geometric shapes are not appropriate. Start with larger shaded drawings at first, done with a dark crayon or large felt pen.

26. Collect examples of line and textural patterns clipped from magazines.

29. Draw tonal figures from life. Pose a model against a plain background. As a readiness activity, project a light against the model and draw the shadow.

Always start with the head. Have students work about the size of the examples shown. Limit poses to 10 – 15 seconds. Work fast. Try for unusual poses. Draw lines for any props used by the models. Keep these shaded figures small. Have a student take quick poses. Urge students to draw smaller if they cannot keep up.

30. Use about a #7 brush for these figures. Start simply with one muddy tone. Puddle a spot for the head, then body, arms and legs. Pose models as with scribble figures. Use one-minute, two-minute poses.

31. Objects can be held beneath a table lamp to achieve the same effect.

32. Have students notice how the illustrations in newspapers and magazines combine tone and contour drawings. These mechanically produced tones are cut by the artist from transparent sheets and are assembled on the drawing.

33. An object's shape can be captured by tearing and taping pieces of newspaper to a background of colored construction paper. Dust lightly with spray paint and remove newspaper and tape. Over this shape, have students do a careful contour drawing of the object. Urge them to allow their drawing to overlap the areas defined by the tone as in the example.

34. Do make slides of outstanding drawings! Project them on a light wall to demonstrate

the effect size has on our perception of art work!

35. Have students examine both black and white and color magazine illustrations with a magnifying glass. Point out the difference between line and halftone reproductions. Study the work of the artist Georges Seurat and discuss his pointilist technique.

36. Sometimes, short vertical or horizontal pen strokes will express the subject better than dots. Whichever the student uses, he or she should follow the direction of the lines in the subject.

37. Subjects of intense interest to students will evoke the best work. Capitalize on this factor. Brainstorm possible subjects with your students.

39. A blind gesture drawing to music is a great way to relax and prepare for an expressive drawing.

40. Gesture drawing is not learned in one class period! Do not worry about recognizable, readable objects.

41. Make gesture drawings from the model. Try gesture drawings of various sizes to determine the size students are comfortable with.

42. Students need many and frequent opportunities to imagine. Help them develop mental images: have them close their eyes, read to them, describe incredible animals, places, and situations. Then, have them describe their mental images in pictures as well as in words. Study the surrealists, Dali, Tanguy, and DeChirico.

44. It is important to allow students with well-developed drawing styles to receive recognition for their unique achievements.

45. Fitting drawings into unusual spaces or onto unusually shaped pieces of paper helps one to understand both distortion and composition.

46. Young students will find a row of 4 or 5 frames printed on a piece of paper helpful in doing their first metamorphic drawings.

47. Obtain Sol Lewitt's catalog from the Museum of Modern Art in New York.

   Have students plan a conceptual drawing of their own. Ask the entire class to make the same drawing and discuss the results.

49. Students need to see as many examples of drawings as possible, from all periods and in a variety of styles.

50. It is important to identify students who create unusual images. It is also important that both student and parent understand the potential of the child's talent.

51. A number of computer programs are available that allow images to be created easily. Of course, the trick is for the student to write the program. Slides can be taken of the computer screen if no printer is available.

ISBN 0-9616161-0-5 8.95